THE
CHRISTMAS EVE
GHOST

For Alice

First U.S. edition 2010

Library of Congress Cataloging-in-Publication Data

Hughes, Shirley, date.

The Christmas Eve ghost / Shirley Hughes. —1st U.S. ed.

p.   cm.

Summary: In 1930s Liverpool, England, Bronwen and Dylan live with their widowed mother, who works
long hours doing other people's washing, and even though she sometimes must leave the children alone in
the house, she cautions them not to speak to the O'Rileys next door, who go to a different church.

ISBN 978-0-7636-4472-7

[1. Laundry—Fiction. 2. Single-parent families—Fiction. 3. Prejudices—Fiction. 4. Christmas—Fiction.
5. England—Fiction. 6. Great Britain—History—George VI, 1936–1952—Fiction.]   I. Title.

PZ7.H87395Ch 2010

[E]—dc22   2009051506

10 11 12 13 14 15 LEO 10 9 8 7 6 5 4 3 2 1   NOV 1 0

Printed in Heshan, Guangdong, China

This book was typeset in Mrs. Eaves. The illustrations were done in ink and watercolor.

Candlewick Press
99 Dover Street
Somerville, Massachusetts 02144

visit us at www.candlewick.com

THE CHRISTMAS EVE GHOST

Shirley Hughes

CANDLEWICK PRESS

Once, in the old seaport city of Liverpool, when tramcars clanged up and down the main streets on iron tracks, there lived two children named Bronwen and Dylan.

They had not lived there very long. Mam had brought them there from their village in Wales after Da had died.

Da had been killed in a mining accident when he was working deep underground. Bronwen could just remember his strong arms and his smell of coal dust. But Dylan was too little to remember him at all.

Mam earned a living for the three of them by doing other people's laundry. There were no washing machines in those days, and it was very hard work.

She did not have enough money to pay someone to look after Bronwen and Dylan, so early in the morning before it was light, she had to leave them while they were still asleep.

She pushed the big old pram uphill to the better part of the city where the well-off people lived to collect their dirty laundry.

Mam hurried from house to house, delivering the clean washing and piling up the pram with dirty sheets and towels and shirts and pillowcases.

Then she ran back as fast as she could, worrying and fretting all the way because she hated having to leave the children all alone in the house.

But somehow she always managed to get back before they woke up, just in time to make their breakfast porridge.

As soon as she had cleared the breakfast dishes, Mam set to work.

At the back of the house was a narrow room with a stone floor, called a washhouse. In it were a sink, a washtub, and a big iron mangle for wringing out the wet washing.

In the corner was a little brick fireplace with an iron door, and above it was a metal basin with a wooden lid. This was called a copper.

Bronwen and Dylan watched as Mam lit the fire with sticks and newspaper and put bits of coal on top. Then she filled the basin with cold water from the sink and put the lid on.

When the water was hot, Mam pushed the sheets and towels into the basin with soap flakes and began to boil them clean.

Then she stood bent over her washtub, rubbing and scrubbing at the smaller things with a bar of yellow soap while the washhouse filled up with steam.

When all the things were properly clean, she rinsed them in the sink.

After that she wrung them through the big iron mangle.

Sometimes Bronwen and Dylan helped to turn the big wheel, which worked the rollers that squeezed out the water.

It made them feel very big and strong, turning and turning that wheel for Mam. You had to be careful not to pinch your fingers in the rollers as the laundry went through.

The gray, sudsy water drained into a big tub underneath. When that was done, Mam emptied the tub in the backyard.

If the weather was fine she carried all the laundry outside in big baskets and pegged it out on the clothesline to dry.

But if it rained she dried it in the kitchen, draped over wooden frames called clotheshorses or raised up to the ceiling on a pulley. On those days Bronwen and Dylan ate their dinner among the wet sheets.

Next came the ironing. There was no electricity in their house, so Mam heated up her iron over the kitchen stove. She had to take great care not to make it too hot in case it scorched the linens. That would have been a great disaster. When it was all finished and aired, she folded it beautifully and piled it neatly in the old pram, ready to push it back up the hill early the next morning.

Mam was a big sturdy woman, but she did get very tired, and she hated the city dirt.

In the evenings she was mostly too tired to do anything but sit in her chair and look into the fire, remembering the green valley where she had lived as a child and wishing that they were all back there again.

Sometimes she told Bronwen and Dylan thrilling stories about dragons and hauntings and wicked devils with tails and ghosties that came down the chimney at night.

On fine days Bronwen and Dylan hopped and skipped and played some great games with the other children in the street.

On Saturday nights they had a bath in a tin tub in front of the kitchen fire.

And on Sundays they put on their best clothes and went with Mam to sing hymns in Chapel.

In the house next to theirs lived
Mr. and Mrs. O'Riley and their two
handsome sons.

Mr. O'Riley worked at the docks,
unloading great bales of goods from
the holds of ships that had come
into the port from all over the world.

The O'Riley boys worked there too,
alongside their dad. They set out very
early in the morning with all the other
men, *tramp, tramp, tramping* along the
cobbled street.

In the bad times there was no work
for them and no money either, and
they had to stand idle on the street
corner, whiling away the day as
best they could.

Mam never spoke to the O'Rileys except to say "Good morning."

"We keep ourselves to ourselves," she told Bronwen and Dylan. And that meant that they were not to speak to the O'Rileys either.

Bronwen thought it was very strange. There was nothing wrong with the O'Rileys as far as she could see.

But, of course, she did as Mam told her.

The O'Rileys did not go to Chapel. They went to another church. Once Bronwen had peeked inside and seen beautiful statues and colored glass and candles all alight.

She thought it looked lovely, much prettier than their plain chapel with its whitewashed walls. But when she asked Mam if they could go there one Sunday, just for a change, Mam's face became very stern and serious. She told Bronwen that the church was for a different sort of people, not their kind, and that she was never to look in there again.

Christmas was coming, but times were bad and there was no money
to spare. Mam was working long hours to save a little extra to buy
something nice for Bronwen and Dylan.

At last, on Christmas Eve, all the extra laundry was finished and folded
into the pram. Bronwen and Dylan went with Mam, delivering it to all
the houses.

On the way home they saw the brightly lit shops with dead rabbits and
turkeys and joints of meat hanging up and people selling toys in the street
and piles of apples on market carts.

Bronwen and Dylan were tired because they had walked so far, so Mam
took them home.

But she still had more shopping to do. She did not like to leave the children alone in the house after dark, but this evening she picked up her purse and told them that she was just going to run down to the shop at the end of the street, and that they were to play together like good children until she came back.

"I won't be long," she said. "Don't answer the door if anyone knocks."

After Mam had gone, Bronwen put her dolls to bed, and Dylan watched. She pretended that they were being naughty and not going to sleep until Father Christmas had visited.

Dylan said, "I don't think Father Christmas will come to our house anyway, because if he came down our chimney he'd burn his feet!"

"Perhaps he'll come through the back door," said Bronwen.

And then there came a knock.
It was not the front door knocker.
It was coming from the back
of the house.

And it was more like a plonk
than a knock.

Plonk! it went.

Then

Plonk!

Plonk!

They both sat still and listened.
It came again:

Plonk!

Plonk!

Plonk!

Plonk!

Bronwen got up and crept into the back kitchen. Dylan followed, hanging on to her pinafore.

The noise was coming from the wash-house. It sounded strange and echoing. Bronwen pushed open the door.

There was only a little pale moonlight coming in from the window by the sink.

"Maybe Father Christmas is coming down the washhouse chimney," said Bronwen.

"Don't go in there, Bron. Please don't!" whispered Dylan.

The noise came again, suddenly. It was certainly coming from the dark corner by the copper.

Plonk! Plonk! Plonk!

"Somebody's hiding in the copper," said Bronwen.

"And that somebody's trying to get out! It's not Father Christmas!
It's a horrid ghostie coming down the chimney to get us!" shrieked Dylan.

And he bolted, screaming, through the kitchen, down the hallway
and out into the street.

Bronwen ran after him. She was screaming too.

They did not run far. They fell straight into the arms of Mrs. O'Riley,
who was coming home with the family shopping.

"Glory be! What in the world is all this, then?" she cried,
dumping down her baskets.

After she had calmed Bronwen and Dylan enough to hear their story, she left her shopping and took them each by the hand, and they all marched bravely back into the house. When Mrs. O'Riley came with them to the dark washhouse, it did not seem nearly so frightening. Soon the sound came from behind the copper again:

Plonk! Plonk! Plonk!

"Sure I know what that noise is," said Mrs. O'Riley firmly. "And it's nothing to be afraid of. You'd better come along back to my house until your ma gets back, and then you can see for yourselves."

But first she said that Bronwen must leave a note for Mam in case she was worried about where they were.

So Bronwen found a piece of paper and a stub of pencil and wrote:

Deer Mam
We are gon next dor
lov and × × ×
Bronwen

They propped it up on the mantel beside the clock.

Mrs. O'Riley's house was very different from theirs. In the hallway was a picture of Mary and Baby Jesus with a vase of flowers in front of it. And in the kitchen there were shelves with shining china and brass and a delicious smell of stew.

At the back of the house was a wash-house just like theirs but turned the other way around and brightly lit. In it were the two O'Riley boys and their dad. They had rigged up a dartboard next to the copper and were in the middle of a game.

When they threw a dart it landed on the board—*plonk!*

"That's the noise you were hearing!" Mrs. O'Riley told Bronwen and Dylan kindly. "Sure, and it's nothing but a game of darts! Nothing to be scared of now, is it?"

Bronwen and Dylan stared like two solemn little owls. The O'Riley boys stopped their game and grinned at them.

Mam was very flustered and anxious when she came to fetch them. But she found Bronwen and Dylan sitting happily by the O'Rileys' kitchen fire, eating slices of bread dripping with golden syrup.

"I'm very grateful to you," said Mam to Mrs. O'Riley when she heard all about what had happened. "I blame myself for leaving the children alone, but it's so difficult sometimes . . ."

"Think nothing of it, Mrs. Williams," said Mrs. O'Riley. "I'll be glad to keep an eye on them any time you need to slip out."

Then Mam and Mrs. O'Riley
drank a cup of tea together and
chatted. When it was time to say
good night, they all wished one
another a happy Christmas.

That night, when Bronwen and Dylan had hung their stockings and were safely tucked up in bed, Mam told them to remember Da in their prayers and give thanks for all blessings that Christmas night.

"Can I give thanks for Mrs. O'Riley and Mr. O'Riley and the O'Riley boys too?" asked Dylan.

"Mrs. O'Riley was a big blessing to us when we thought there was a horrid ghostie in the washhouse," added Bronwen.

Mam did not answer for a moment. Her face was very serious and thoughtful. Then she smiled, and it was like the sun coming out over green fields.

"Yes, of course you must," she said.

A NOTE FROM SHIRLEY HUGHES

I always knew that one day I would make a picture book that drew on my vivid childhood memories of Liverpool in the 1930s. The bustling shops, tramcars, and thrilling monumental buildings stood in stark contrast with the cramped squalor of the backstreets, where the struggle to keep clean and make a decent life for a family was very hard.

I found all the domestic details easy to recall. The huge challenge of Monday-morning wash day, with the washing all done by hand, the washtubs, scrubbing boards, mangles, and clotheslines which I well remember, are now for most people mercifully a thing of the past. But the kindness of neighbors like Mrs. O'Riley, who comes to the rescue when Bronwen and Dylan are sure that a ghost is stalking their washhouse, is something we all need and depend upon today as much as ever.

Shirley Hughes